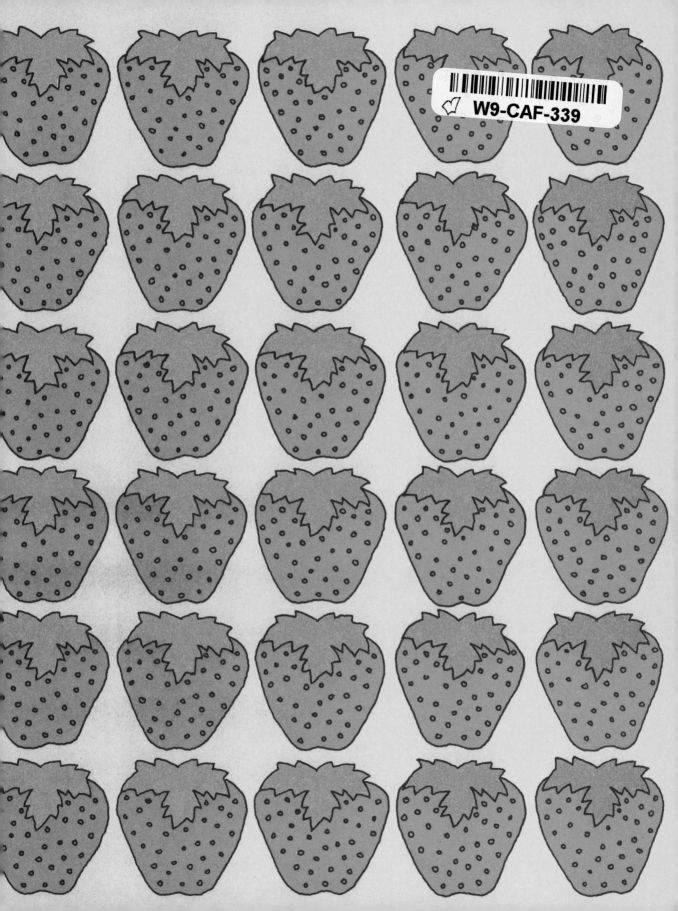

Bedford Stickybear

Sara Stickybear

Bumper Stickybear

this
strawberry library
of first learning
book
belongs to

Library of Congress Cataloging in Publication Data

   Hefter, Richard.
     Fast food.

     (Stickybear books / Richard Hefter)
     Summary: The Stickybears name their new restaurant
Fast Food, but after all their customers leave they decide to
change the name.
     [1. Restaurants, lunch rooms, etc. – Fiction.   2. Bears –
Fiction]   I. Title.   II. Series: Hefter, Richard.   Stickybear
books.
PZ7.H3587Fas   1983   [E]   83-6734
ISBN 0-911787-09-7

fast
food

by Richard Hefter

Optimum Resource, Inc. • Connecticut

It was a bright, sunny morning for the grand opening of the Stickybears' new restaurant.

Bedford finished hanging the sign while Bumper and Sara polished the counter.

The sign said "FAST FOOD."

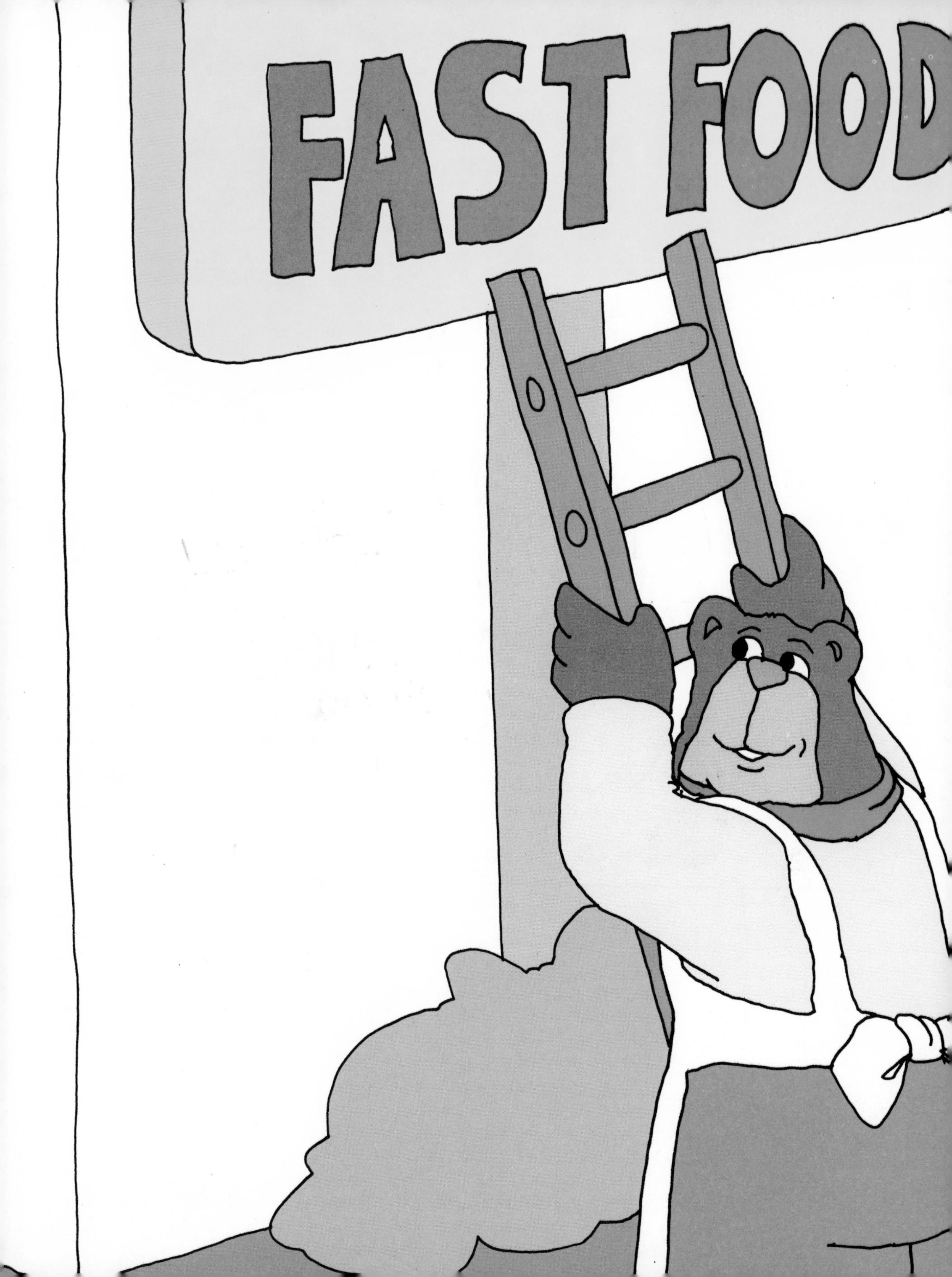
FAST FOOD

"The customers will be arriving soon," smiled Stickybear. "And we have to give them *fast* service because the name of our restaurant is FAST FOOD!"

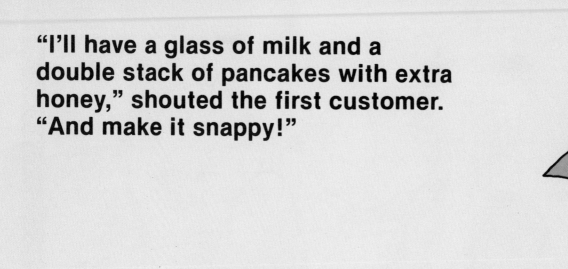

"I'll have a glass of milk and a double stack of pancakes with extra honey," shouted the first customer. "And make it snappy!"

"I'll have toast and soup and a glass of juice and some porridge, hold the honey," said the second customer.

"Make mine a cheese sandwich and tea and honey," growled the third customer. "And make it fast please, I'm very hungry!"

"I'll have two apples and soup and three boiled eggs and bread and honey," grumbled the fourth customer.

"Where are my eggs?" frowned the fourth customer.

"Look out!" gasped the third customer.

"You spilled the honey!" whined the second customer.

"Where's my soup?" shouted
the second customer.

"Hurry up," said all the customers. "We're late! We want our food fast! We can't wait all day."

"We're leaving!" announced the first customer.

All the customers marched out of the restaurant.

"I know," said Bedford.
He grabbed a brush and some
paint and ran outside.

Stickybear painted a big new
sign and hung it up.

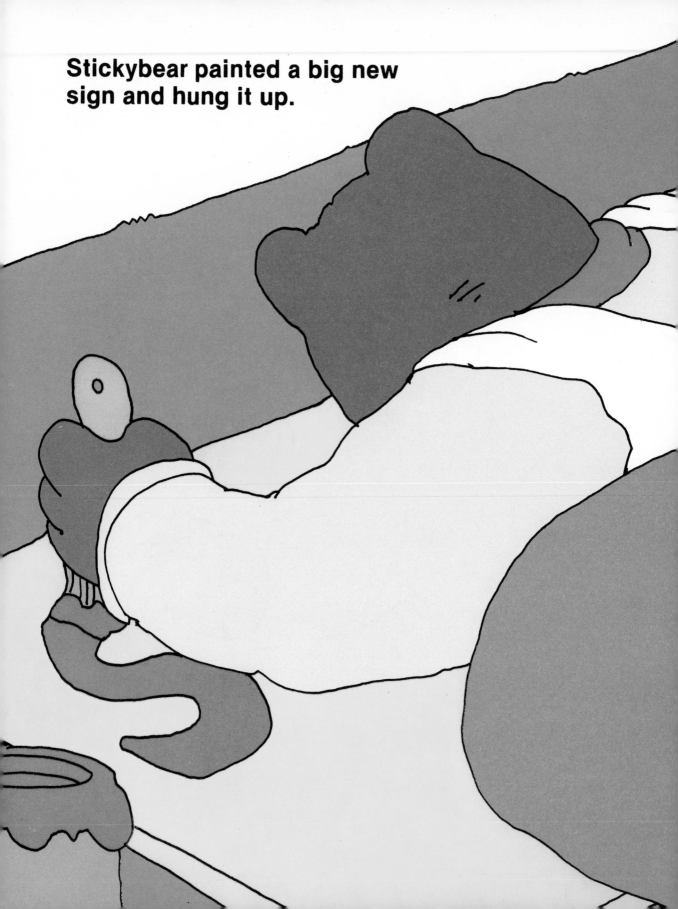

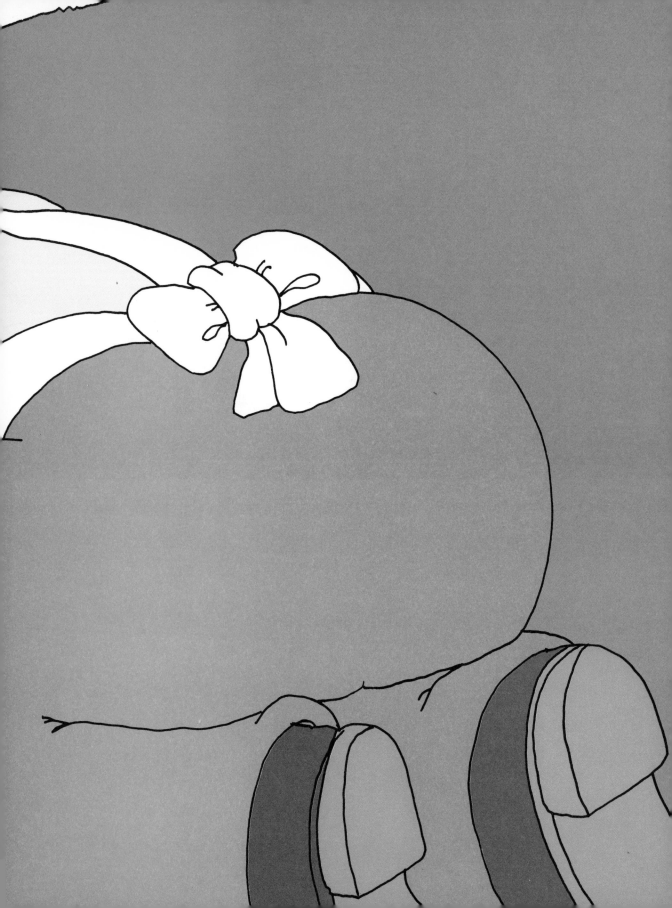

The new sign said "SLOW FOOD."

Bumper ran outside and tacked on another sign.

His sign said "MESSY FOOD."

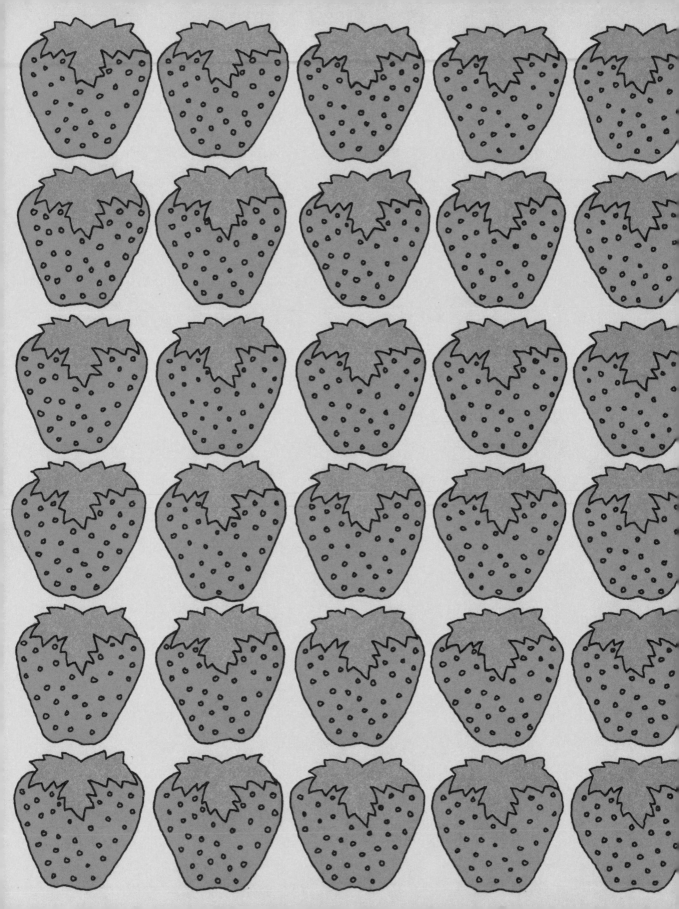